I Am My History

Published by: Brian Keith Harris II
Laurel, MD

Printed in the United States of America

ISBN: 978-0-578-73021-9
Library of Congress Control Number: 2020913435

For more information, visit

www.briankeithharris.com

Dedication

To my Uncle Ron,
Ms. Jean Bryant,
Malcom Andress,
and Lamont Jones Jr.

I am My **History**,
Walking tall, standing in **royalty**.

African Masks

The Great Pyramid of Giza

I am a direct descendant of kings and queens who ruled with grace, wisdom and dignity.

I AM MY HISTORY

6

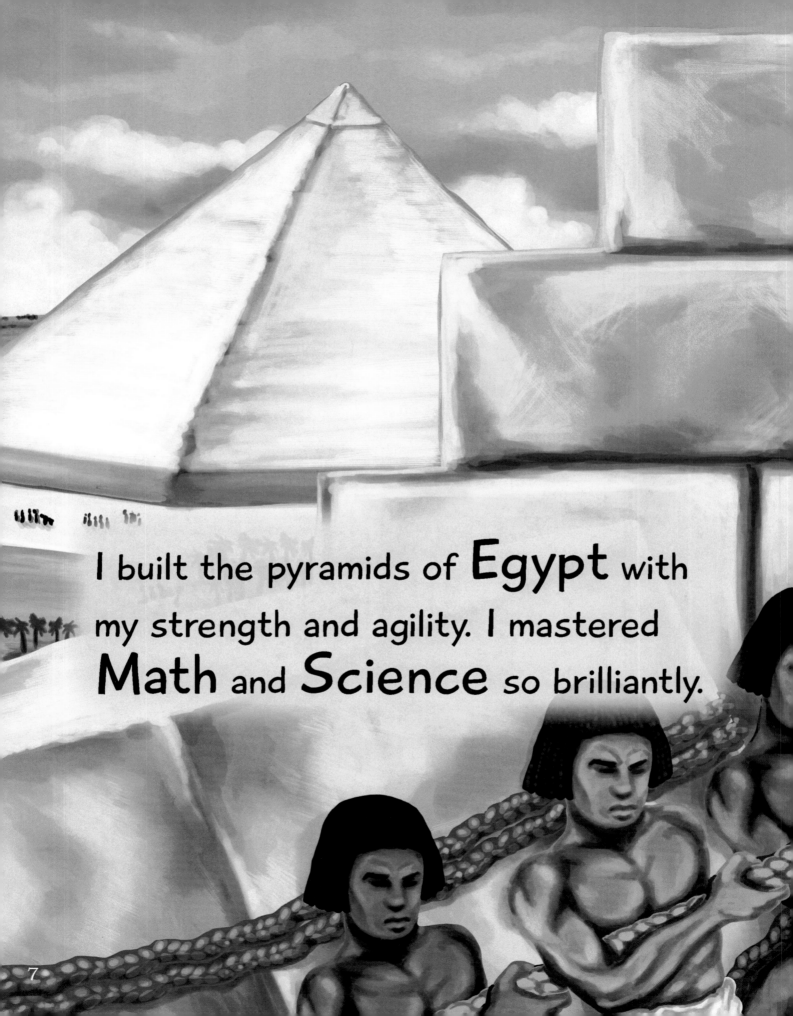

I built the pyramids of **Egypt** with my strength and agility. I mastered **Math** and **Science** so brilliantly.

I am My History,
A child of the **diaspora**
A survivor of **slavery.**

For four hundred years I fought to be **free**, escaping the hands of **hatred** and **captivity**.

I AM a powerful source of peace.

I AM a brave beautiful light.

I AM essential to the Earth.

I AM the glimmering hope in the

darkness of night.

I am my History,
The **injustices** of the world did not
stop me.
I overcame **obstacles** and beat
adversity.

BLACK WALL ST

TULSA 1921

I stood up like **Martin,**

CIVIL RIGHTS

2005

1913

42

Rosa, and Jackie

I AM a vision of My ancestors.

I AM a symbol of Love.

I AM a star in the galaxy.

I AM a gift from above.

I am My History,

Walking tall, standing in royalty.

I will continue with this legacy

knowing that nothing can STOP ME!

ABOUT THE AUTHOR

Brian Keith Harris II is an award-winning educator, lecturer,and motivational speaker, recognized for his work in transforming the landscape for black and brown children through teaching history, poetry, and dance. He is the Founder of Cultivating Young Kings, an organization that provides best practices and training for teachers, school districts, and community leaders who educate and work with black and brown boys in and out of the classroom. He is also the Founder and Artistic Director of Sons of Freedom Dance Institute, an organization that nurtures character, increases social awareness, and builds a spiritual foundation for black and brown boys through classical and contemporary forms of dance and movement.

In 2019, Brian was named one of Black Enterprise Magazine's *BeModern Men of Distinction* for his creativity in teaching black history and culture through modern and lyrical dance.

He is the Director of Outplacement and Graduate Support at Bishop John T. Walker School for Boys, a tuition-free school educating boys in underserved communities in Washington, DC.

Brian is the author of Freedom's Design: 20 Days of Empowering Black Kings and is the father of one son and two godchildren.

ABOUT THE ILLUSTRATOR

CJ LOVE

C.J. Love is a graduate of Maryland Institute College of Art, with a Bachelor of Fine Arts in Graphic Design. He specializes in illustrating, caricatures, and mural painting.
(www.clove2design.com)

A NOTE FROM THE AUTHOR

When I was 12 years old I participated in the Mr. African-American Pageant in my hometown of Pittsburgh, PA. This was not a traditional pageant, but more like a Rites of Passage program for black boys ages 12-18. We met every Saturday for 12 weeks and at the end of that time, we competed for the title of Mr. African-American. This program taught character development, life skills, and black history and culture, while also teaching etiquette and how to 'dress for success.' I remember waking up every Saturday morning, excited and ready to learn about the many Black Americans whose inventions and contributions to our country were forgotten or unrecognized.

I can still remember my first Saturday history class. 13 teenage boys sat in wooden seats (the kind that make noise when you sit down) in an old auditorium looking at a map of Africa. That day, we learned about Ancient Kemet, modern-day Egypt, and how our ancestors built pyramids, created a writing system called hieroglyphics, and used red clay from the Nile River to build homes and tools. I was so enthralled by learning about Ancient Kemet, that I got berated by the other boys for asking too many questions and delaying lunchtime. That was a rich moment of learning about my history and I can't remember another time in my childhood where I had that opportunity again.

I wrote this book to provide each of our children that same feeling of excitement and joy I felt over 20 years ago learning about Black history and culture. It is my sincere hope that as they read each line, they will be empowered and inspired by our ancestors and they will realize that they have the same creativity, intelligence, and resilience as those who came before them.

Young Queen and King,
You ARE YOUR History, so shine on!

-Brian